This ~~book~~ **octopus!** belongs to...

All I Want is an Octopus

An original concept by author Tracy Gunaratnam

© Tracy Gunaratnam

Illustrated by Valentina Fontana

MAVERICK ARTS PUBLISHING LTD

Studio 11, City Business Centre, 6 Brighton Road, Horsham, West Sussex, RH13 5BB, +44 (0)1403 256941

© Maverick Arts Publishing Limited 2021

Published October 2021

First Published in the UK in 2021 by MAVERICK ARTS PUBLISHING LTD

American edition published in 2021 by Maverick Arts Publishing, distributed in the United States and Canada by Lerner Publishing Group Inc., 241 First Avenue North, Minneapolis, MN 55401 USA

ISBN 978-1-84886-779-6

Maverick
publishing
www.maverickbooks.co.uk

distributed by **Lerner**™

All I Want is an Octopus

Written by
Tracy Gunaratnam

Illustrated by
Valentina Fontana

For Cath and Ben with love. T.G.

Pets as you know come in all **SHAPES** and **SIZES**.

Some are quite scruffy while others win prizes.

Some sit in **HANDBAGS** and some **RIDE THE BUS.**

But all I want is an...

...OCTOPUS!

"An **OCTOPUS**," said Dad. "Goodness me.
A creature like that belongs in the sea."

"But DAAAAAAAAAAAAAAAaaaaaaaD!"

"My octopus would **WASH** your car.
He'd **PAINT** the house and **PLAY GUITAR**."

"Oh wow," said Dad. "He's helpful and fun.
I'll leave that decision up to your **MOM**."

So... I asked my mom and here's what she said.
"Don't be so **SILLY!** Get ready for bed!"

OOOOOOOOOOOOOOOOOOOOOM!"

"My octopus would make you **LAUGH.**

He'd **STYLE** your hair...

...AND run your bath."

"Really," said Mom. "Then maybe we can...
But first we'll need to ask your **GRAN**."

"An octopus," said Gran. "Yippee! Sounds like a super idea to me..."

"He'll roller skate and jump in puddles...

...Play mini golf and give wonderful cuddles."

"Gran," I said. "You're right! It's true!
Would you like to have one too?"

"An octopus sounds great," said Gran.

"But nothing tops an...